An I Can R[illegible]Book™



# Gran[illegible] Trick-or-Treat



story and pictures by

**Emily Arnold McCully**

HarperTrophy®
*An Imprint of* HarperCollins*Publishers*

*To the Loughridge Girls*



Grandmas Trick-or-Treat

www.harperchildrens.com

Library of Congress Cataloging-in-Publication Data
McCully, Emily Arnold.
Grandmas trick-or-treat / by Emily Arnold McCully.
p. cm. — (An I can read book)
Summary: Pip's two grandmothers, who cannot agree on anything, take Pip and her friends trick-or-treating on Halloween.
ISBN 0-06-028730-6 — ISBN 0-06-028731-4 (lib. bdg.) — ISBN 0-06-444277-2 (pbk.)
[1. Halloween—Fiction. 2. Grandmothers—Fiction. 3. Bullies—Fiction.] I. Title. II. Series.
PZ7.M13913 Gp 2001 00-039720
[E]—dc21

First Harper Trophy Edition, 2002
❖

# Contents

# Chapter One

On Halloween,
Grandma Nan came to baby-sit
Pip and her friend Ski.

"Look, Pip," Grandma Nan said,

"I made a costume for you!"

She pulled it over Pip's head.

"No thanks, I made my own,"

Pip said.

"This one is perfect!"

said Grandma Nan.

"You look funny as an angel!"

said Ski.

The doorbell rang.

“There’s nobody there,” said Pip.

“How rude!” said Grandma Nan.

The doorbell rang again.

Pip went to open it.

“Nobody’s th—” she started to say.

"Boo! Boo! Boo! Boo!"

"Oh my!" said Grandma Nan.

“Grandma Sal!” said Pip.

“Just keeping you on your toes,” said Grandma Sal.

“That was childish, Sal!” said Grandma Nan.

“Relax, Nan. It’s Halloween!”

said Grandma Sal.

“You look silly,” Grandma Nan said.

"Ski, you look really scary,"

said Grandma Sal.

"Thanks," said Ski.

"I want to scare Big Bertha."

Pip said, "Last Halloween that bully

and her friends chased us

and took Mona's treat bag!"

"Halloween can bring out

the worst in people,"

said Grandma Nan.

"But it's so much fun!"

said Grandma Sal.

"Here, I have a witch hat

and cape for you, Nan!"

"No, thank you,"

said Grandma Nan.

"We are grown-ups, Sal."

“I will bring them just in case,”

said Grandma Sal.

“I have fangs, too.

Want them, Pip?”

“I have my own costume!”

Pip shouted. She put it on.

“I’m a pencil,” she said.

“Terrific,” said Grandma Sal.

“Let’s go!”

# Chapter Two

The gang was waiting on the corner.
"What kind of a costume is that?"
asked Mona.
"I'm not wearing a costume!"
said Grandma Nan.

"Is everyone ready
to play some tricks?"
asked Grandma Sal.

“The children will not play tricks,”

said Grandma Nan.

“They will have good manners.

Children, be polite.”

“Be scary,” said Grandma Sal.

Grandma Nan marched up to a house and pressed the doorbell.

“Good evening, madam,” she said.

“Pip, do you have something to say?”

“Trick or treat,” said Pip.

The woman gave them all candy.

“What do you say?”

asked Grandma Nan.

“Thank you!” they all said.

“Now form a line,”

said Grandma Nan,

“and save your treats for later.”

"You kids aren't very scary,"
said Grandma Sal.
"Watch me this time."

Grandma Sal rang a doorbell.

A man opened the door.

"Boo!" yelled Grandma Sal.

"Eek!" said the man.

He slammed the door.

"Now, that's scary!"

said Grandma Sal.

"But we didn't get any treats!"

said Mona.

"I will ring the next bell,"

said Grandma Nan.

"No, I will!" said Grandma Sal.

Pip and Ski stayed back.

"Grandma Nan's good manners

and Grandma Sal's tricks

are driving me crazy!" said Pip.

"We aren't having any fun at all,"
Ski said. "It's time
to trick the grandmas!
Let's tell the other kids."
At the next house,
the grandmas went to the door
together and pressed the bell.
The door opened,
and a man peered out.
"Nan? Sal?" the man asked.
"Aren't you a little old for
trick-or-treating?"

"We are baby-sitting!"

said Grandma Nan.

"I don't see any babies," said the man.

"I suppose you want some treats."

"Certainly not!" said Grandma Nan.

“What have you got?”

asked Grandma Sal.

The man gave her some candy

and closed the door.

Grandma Nan said,

“Now let’s find those kids!”

## Chapter Three

The kids ran down the street
and cut across a yard.
At last, Pip said, “Slow down.
I’m out of breath.”
“We’ve lost the grandmas,”
said Ski.

"But where are we?" asked Julio.

The street was quiet and dark.

"There's no one at home here,"
said Mona.

"What was that sound?" asked Ski.

"It was just dried leaves,"

said Julio.

"It's spooky," said Pip.

They walked close together.

"Are we lost?" asked Norman.

"EEEEEYYYYOWWWW!" someone yelled, and a pirate jumped in front of them.

“It’s Bertha!” Pip shouted.

“Run for it!”

Then they saw two more pirates.

"Got you!" said Bertha.

"Don't move, or we will spray

you with rotten-egg juice!
Hand over those treat bags!
Now!"

Suddenly
there was a terrible scream,
and two huge monsters
came out of the dark.
"What's that?"
cried Bertha.

The monsters jumped at the bullies.

"Let's get out of here!"

yelled the pirates.

"Wait for me!" cried Bertha.

"Quick! Run the other way,"

shouted Julio.

"Wait!" said Pip.

"Those monsters look familiar."

“The grandmas!” said Ski.

"Wow!" said Mona. "You were great!
You really scared those bullies."
"They needed a lesson
in manners," said Grandma Nan.

"Speaking of manners,"
said Grandma Sal,
"aren't you kids
forgetting something?"
"Thank you, Grandmas!"
said the kids.
"You're welcome,"
said Grandma Nan.
"I had something else in mind,"
said Grandma Sal.
"Treats!" said Pip.
"We'd be happy to share!"
"Goody," said Grandma Nan.

"Halloween sure does bring out the best in people, doesn't it, Sal?" Grandma Nan said.

"You bet!" said Grandma Sal.